W9-BSL-805

When the Rain Stops

To Ralph, Jill, Tiana, and Anneka Norgren,
and to rainy days at "the house" together—S.C.

To Bud and Evelyne Johnson—H.S.

 Inquiries should be addressed to Lothrop, Lee & Shepard Books, a division of William Morrow & Company, Inc., 1350 Avenue of the Americas, New York, New York 10019. Printed in the United States of America.
First Edition 1 2 3 4 5 6 7 8 9 10

Library of Congress Cataloging in Publication Data
Cole, Sheila. When the rain stops / by Sheila R. Cole ; illustrated by Henri Sorensen.
p. cm. Summary: After a downpour a little girl and her father go out to pick blackberries, encountering a variety of wildlife on the way. ISBN 0-688-07654-8. — ISBN 0-688-07655-6 (lib. bdg.)
[1. Rain and rainfall—Fiction.] I. Sorensen, Henri, ill. II. Title. PZ7.C67353Wg 1991 [E]—dc20
90-19124 CIP AC

When the Rain Stops

BY SHEILA COLE

ILLUSTRATED BY HENRI SORENSEN

LOTHROP, LEE & SHEPARD BOOKS NEW YORK

It was cloudy when Leila and Daddy went out to gather blackberries for a pie. *Que-ee, que-ee,* a blackbird called from a tree. A rabbit darted out in front of them and disappeared under a bush.

Deer tensed, then lifted their heads to sniff at the wind.

A fox crept through the tall meadow grass looking for a mouse to eat.

The sky grew darker. Leaves trembled in the breeze. Leila heard the rumble of thunder. She felt a raindrop on her cheek and another on her nose.

Then all at once, the rain was coming down hard.

The blackbird huddled under the leaves, trying to stay dry. The rabbit crouched under a bush.

The deer dashed into the woods, where trees would shelter them. The fox trotted off to hide in its den.

Leila and Daddy ran all the way home.

They peeled off their wet clothes as soon as they were inside the door and hung them in the bathroom to dry. Daddy gave Leila a towel to dry herself with and sent her to her room to change. When she came back, there was a cup of hot chocolate waiting for her.

The rain drummed *plippetyplippetyplippetyplip-pety* on the roof. It beat *rat-a-tat-tat-tat* against the windows. Outside, a car *swish-swished* along the wet road. Down came the rain, turning the earth to mud and feeding the thirsty roots of plants.

In the house, all warm and dry, Leila took out her markers. She was drawing a picture of a squirrel in a tree when she heard *plip, plip, plop*. She looked up to see water dripping from the ceiling onto the floor.

"Daddy," she called, "it's raining in here."

The drops fell harder and faster.

"So it is," said Daddy.

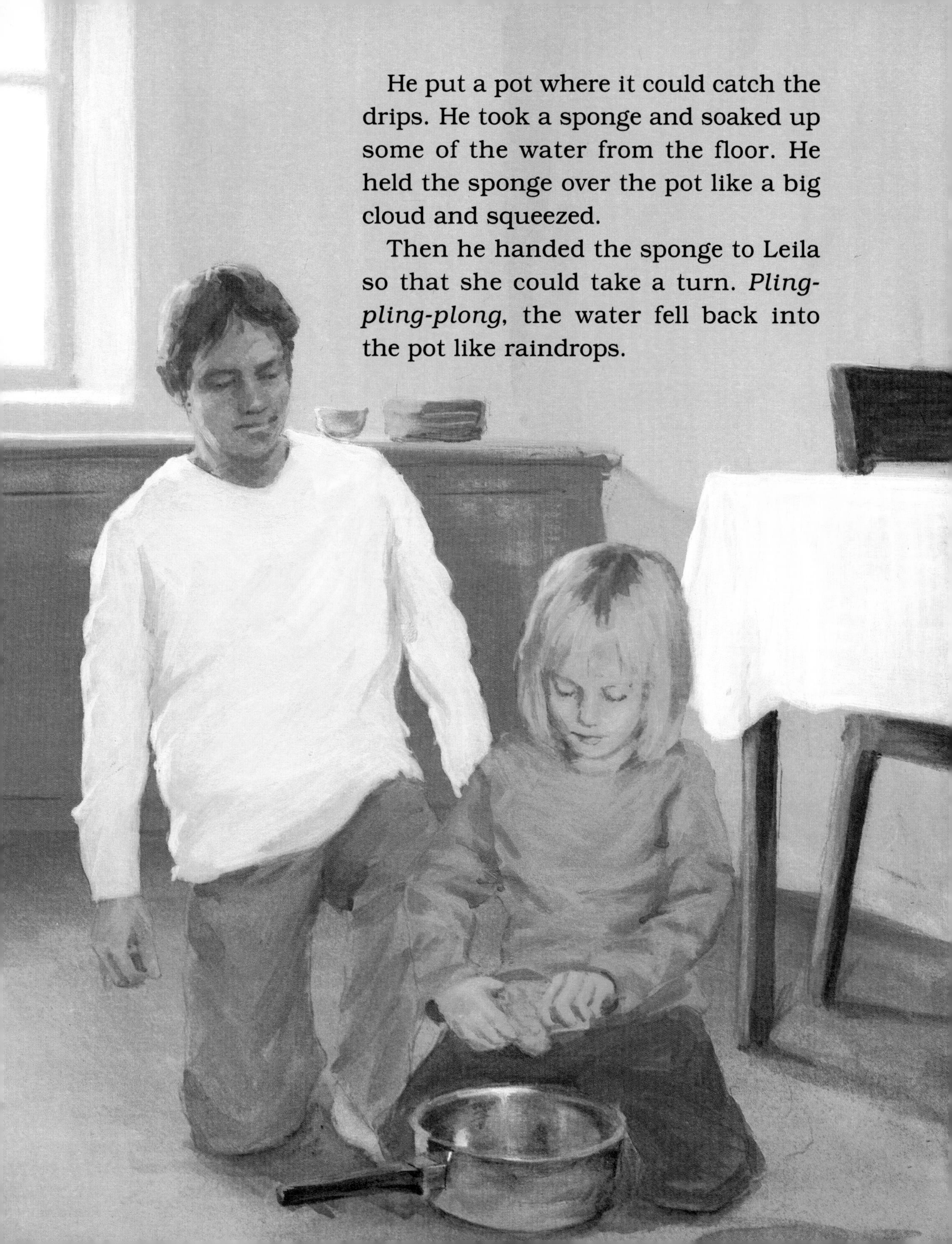

He put a pot where it could catch the drips. He took a sponge and soaked up some of the water from the floor. He held the sponge over the pot like a big cloud and squeezed.

Then he handed the sponge to Leila so that she could take a turn. *Pling-pling-plong*, the water fell back into the pot like raindrops.

After a while, the rain stopped falling, but everything was still wet. Water *drip-dropped* from the trees and bushes onto the ground and collected in puddles. It ran in trickles and rivulets into the brook, which gurgled and chortled as it rushed along. It swelled the pond. Inside, water still dripped from the ceiling into the pot. *Plip-plop, plip-plop*.

A breeze blew the clouds away. The sun broke out bright and warm. The water from the puddles and rivulets, from the pond and the brook, from the rooftops and roads, slowly began to dry up, sinking into the ground and evaporating into the air. Inside, the water dripped from the ceiling more and more slowly, *plip, plip...plip, plip...plip...plip*, until it stopped.

By and by, the moisture in the air would gather together into clouds. Someday, it would again fall to the ground as rain. But for now, the rain was over.

Leila and Daddy put on their boots and went out a second time with their blackberry pails. They walked through the wet meadow grass, *squish-squash, squish-squash*.

A rabbit raced across the wet meadow, raising a mist that glittered in the sun.

Worms crawled out of the wet earth. Insects swarmed in the air. Birds chirped and twittered from every bush and tree as they enjoyed the feast.

Peepers sang from all the puddles.

A mouse crept out of its burrow to nibble on the tender grass.

One squirrel chased another along the branches of an old oak tree.

A woodpecker was *rat-a-tat-tatting, rat-a-tat-tatting*, drilling a tree for insects.

Leila and Daddy looked and looked. They didn't see the deer in the meadow or in the woods, but they knew they were somewhere nearby.

They didn't see any foxes either, because foxes don't hunt in bright sunlight.

But as they were putting the last berries into their pails, they did see a blackbird land on a blackberry bush. *Que-ee, que-ee*, it called.

"He's come to feast on blackberries, too," said Daddy.

"But not on blackberry pie!" said Leila.

"No," said Daddy, "and we won't be eating any pie, either, if we don't go home now and start baking it."